SO-CFK-558

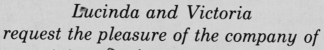

Lucinda and Victoria
request the pleasure of the company of

Liza & liviya Burns

at a tea party
in the Dolls' House
on Wednesday at 4 pm

The Dolls' House   RSVP
The Nursery

For Hannah Keleshian Bawden with love. JB

For Evelyn King with love from her Granddaughter. HP

Special thanks to Hamleys of Regent St Ltd
for allowing the Photographer to have the pick of the store
to select the dolls used in this book.

Text copyright © 1989 Juliet Bawden
Photographs © 1989 Helen Pask
First published 1989 by Blackie and Son Ltd

All rights reserved. No part of this publication may be
reproduced, stored in a retrieval system, or transmitted
in any form or by any means, electronic, mechanical,
photocopying, recording or otherwise without the
written permission of the Publishers.

British Library Cataloguing in Publication Data

Bawden, Juliet
The doll's tea party
I. Title   II. Pask, Helen
823'.914 [J]

ISBN 0-216-92475-8

Blackie and Son Ltd
7 Leicester Place
London WC2H 7BP

First American edition published in 1989
by Peter Bedrick Books, New York

Library of Congress Cataloging-in-Publication Data

Bawden, Juliet
The dolls' tea party/text by Juliet Bawden;
photographs by Helen Pask.
p.   cm.
Summary: Feeling bored, Lucinda decides to give
a tea party for all the dolls in the nursery.
ISBN 0-87226-413-0
(1. Dolls—Fiction.   2. Parties—Fiction.)
I. Pask, Helen, ill.   II. Titles.
PZ7.B329Do 1989
(E)—dc19   89-6577

Printed in Portugal

The Dolls' Tea Party

Text by Juliet Bawden
Photographs by Helen Pask

Blackie
London

Bedrick/Blackie
New York

Lucinda, the oldest doll in the nursery, had been feeling bored.

Nothing ever happens here, she thought. I know, I shall have a tea party. I'm sure Victoria would come and help me. I shall ask all the dolls in the nursery, even that naughty Violet Louise. Of course Teddy must come too.

She sat down by the parlour window and wrote out the invitations.

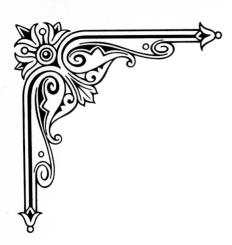

A short time later Victoria arrived. The two friends sat down together, Lucinda with a cookery book and Victoria with her quill, ink and paper.

'What shall we bake?' Lucinda asked her friend.

'Whatever it is, there must be plenty of it. You know how greedy some of the dolls are, and Teddy is famous for his large appetite,' said Victoria.

'Let's make shortbread and Chelsea buns and cakes and chocolate and—' said Lucinda.

'And Bath buns and fruit salad and, of course, tea,' interrupted Victoria.

The friends took the largest basket
they could find on their shopping
expedition. They bought flour, sugar,
butter, chocolate, fruit and bread.

Victoria also called in at the florists
and bought a bunch of red roses for
Lucinda.

The dolls arrived back at the nursery
quite exhausted but they went straight
into the kitchen to prepare the tea.

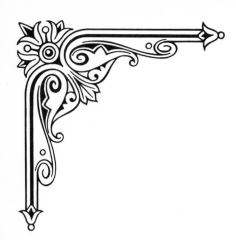

The dolls washed their hands and put on their aprons.

Victoria mixed together flour, butter and sugar to make shortbread and then rolled out the mixture. Lucinda made the fruit salad and buns and cut the french sticks into pieces.

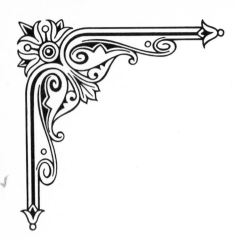

When all the food was prepared,
Lucinda put her best crocheted
tablecloth on the table. Victoria
brought in the best china cups and
saucers. They were white with a pretty
blue rim and a pink rose pattern.

'Oh dear! I'm not sure everyone will
fit round this table,' she said.

'Let's set the small table for the little
dolls,' suggested Lucinda.

At last, all the preparations were complete. The tables were laid and the two dolls had taken off their aprons and caps and brushed their hair.

There was a knock at the door. The dolls and Teddy had arrived. Jessica Rose brought a beautiful basket of dried flowers for her hostess.

Naughty Violet Louise rushed over to the table to look at the food!

The dolls sat down to eat. Lucinda said, 'I'll be mother,' and she poured the tea.

The dolls thought the food was delicious and congratulated Lucinda and Victoria.

Violet Louise, who was a rather fidgety
doll, rocked backwards on her chair.
She rocked slightly harder than she
meant and tipped up backwards,
knocking the table as she fell. A cup of
hot tea spilled on to Teddy who was so
shocked he fell on the floor in surprise.

Lucinda and Jessica Rose helped Teddy
up. Jessica Rose bandaged his leg.
Victoria and Emma told Violet Louise
what a naughty doll she was and how
thoughtless she had been.

Poor Violet Louise felt quite upset.
She offered to clear the table to show
how sorry she was.

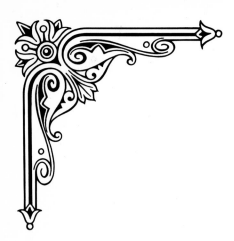

Jessica Rose, who was kind hearted,
offered to help Violet Louise, so the
two small dolls cleared the table.
However, as soon as they were in the
kitchen, Violet Louise, who could never
be good for long, started to eat all the
food that was left over.

The dolls decided it was time to play,
so Teddy and Emma looked at
Lucinda's photograph album. There
were photographs that her sailor
brother had sent her from the far off
lands he had visited. Lucinda and
Victoria played a game of snap.

At last it was time for the dolls to go home. Everyone said goodbye to Lucinda. They had enjoyed the tea party very much and were sad to be going home.

'We must do it again,' said Lucinda as she wished goodbye to her friends.